D

D0116879

What Will I Do Without You?

For Cass, the very best of friends—S.G.

For Bertie, William, and Maksymilian—P.D.

KINGFISHER
Larousse Kingfisher Chambers Inc.
95 Madison Avenue
New York, New York 10016

First published in 1999
2 4 6 8 10 9 7 5 3
2TR/0600/TWP/REP(REP)/170NMA

LIBRARY OF CONGRESS CATALOGING-IN-PUBLICATION DATA
Grindley, Sally.
What will I do without you? / by Sally Grindley: illustrated by
Penny Dann.—1st ed.
p. cm.
Summary: Figgy Twosocks sulks when her friend Jefferson Bear goes
away to hibernate, but in time she finds a new friend in Hoptail the
squirrel and is able to play again with Jefferson after winter ends.
[1. Foxes Fiction. 2. Bears Fiction. 3. Hibernation Fiction.
4. Friendship Fiction. 5. Squirrels Fiction. 6. Winter Fiction.]
I. Dann, Penny, ill. II. Title.
PZ7.G88446Wgf 1999
[E]—dc21 99-21320 CIP

ISBN 0-7534-5110-7

Printed in Singapore

What Will I Do Without You?

Sally Grindley
Illustrated by Penny Dann

KING*f*ISHER

NEW YORK

Winter was on its way. Jefferson Bear was fat and his fur wobbled more than ever.

"Shall we go for our walk?" asked Figgy Twosocks.

"No time to walk, Figgy," said Jefferson Bear.
"I need to eat. I'm getting ready to hibernate."
"What's hibernate?" asked Figgy.
"Hibernate is what big brown bears
do in the winter," said Jefferson Bear.
"It's when I go to sleep and
don't wake up until spring."

"But what will I do without you?" asked Figgy.
"I'll be back before you know it," said Jefferson Bear.
"I don't want you to go," sulked Figgy Twosocks.

The air turned frosty.

"Time for bed," yawned Jefferson Bear.

"Don't go yet," said Figgy Twosocks.

"I'm sorry little friend—
a big brown bear needs his sleep."

Jefferson Bear hugged her tightly and
disappeared into his cave.
"I'll miss you, JB," called Figgy.

The next morning, it was snowing. Figgy had never seen snow before. She ran to tell Jefferson Bear.

ZZz zzz zzz!

"JB, are you asleep yet?" she called.
A rumbly snore echoed from deep
inside his cave.

Figgy kicked at the snow.
"What good is snow when your
best friend isn't there to share it?"

BIFF! BIFF! BIFF!

Figgy's brothers were
having a snowball fight.

"Can I play?" Figgy Twosocks asked.
"If you want," said Big Smudge.

"Take this!" said Floppylugs.

BIFF!

"Stop it!" Figgy squealed. "That hurts."
"You wanted to play," they said,
and ran off laughing.
"You wouldn't do that if JB
were here," she cried.

Then Figgy Twosocks
had an idea . . . .

All day long she pushed and patted the snow.

All day long she rolled and scooped and shaped it.

Finally, she found
three black stones and
a little twig.

She stood back.

"Every time I look at my
Big White Snow Bear, I will
think of JB," she said.

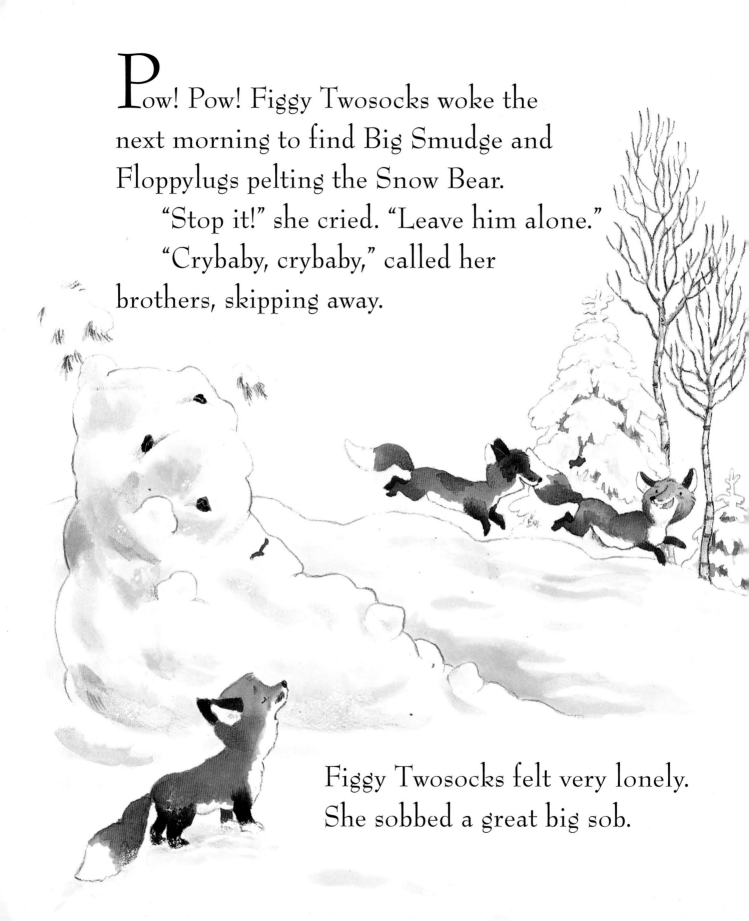

Pow! Pow! Figgy Twosocks woke the next morning to find Big Smudge and Floppylugs pelting the Snow Bear.

"Stop it!" she cried. "Leave him alone."

"Crybaby, crybaby," called her brothers, skipping away.

Figgy Twosocks felt very lonely. She sobbed a great big sob.

Then she began to feel cross.
If JB was her friend, how could
he leave her for so long?
    PIFF!—she threw a snowball
at the Snow Bear.
    PIFF!—and another.
And another—PIFF!

"Hey, don't do that. You'll ruin it," called a voice.

It was Hoptail the squirrel.

"JB's not my friend anymore,"
said Figgy Twosocks.

"Why not?" asked Hoptail.

"He's not here when I
need him."

"But he needs his sleep,"
said Hoptail. "And I need some
help. I have to find the nuts
I buried in the fall."

Hoptail pointed to places where she thought her food was hidden.

Figgy Twosocks dug down through the snow. "One for you!" she squealed, each time she dug up a nut.

"One for me!" she squealed, each time she dug up a worm.

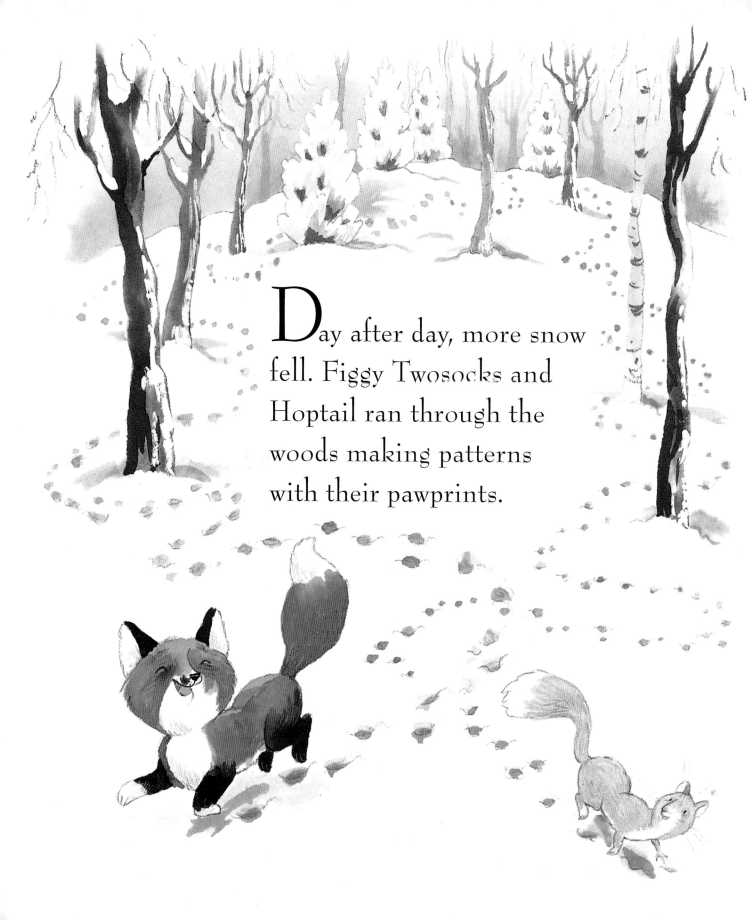

Day after day, more snow
fell. Figgy Twosocks and
Hoptail ran through the
woods making patterns
with their pawprints.

They broke off icicles
and watched them melt
through their paws.

And together they
rebuilt the Big White
Snow Bear.

At the end of each day, Figgy Twosocks went to see the Big White Snow Bear.
"I hope JB won't mind my having another friend," she said.

L̲ittle by little, the days grew warmer.

"The Snow Bear is melting!" cried Figgy.
"What's happening?"
"Spring is coming," said Hoptail.

POW!   POW!

Suddenly, Big Smudge and Floppylugs appeared.

They clambered
onto the Snow Bear
and pushed—
HEAVE . . .

WHOOSH!

The head of the Snow Bear
rolled down the hill.

GRRR!

"OUCH! That hurt," growled a
great big voice.

Big Smudge and Floppylugs ran away.

There was Jefferson Bear, rubbing his nose.
"That's a fine welcome back," he said.

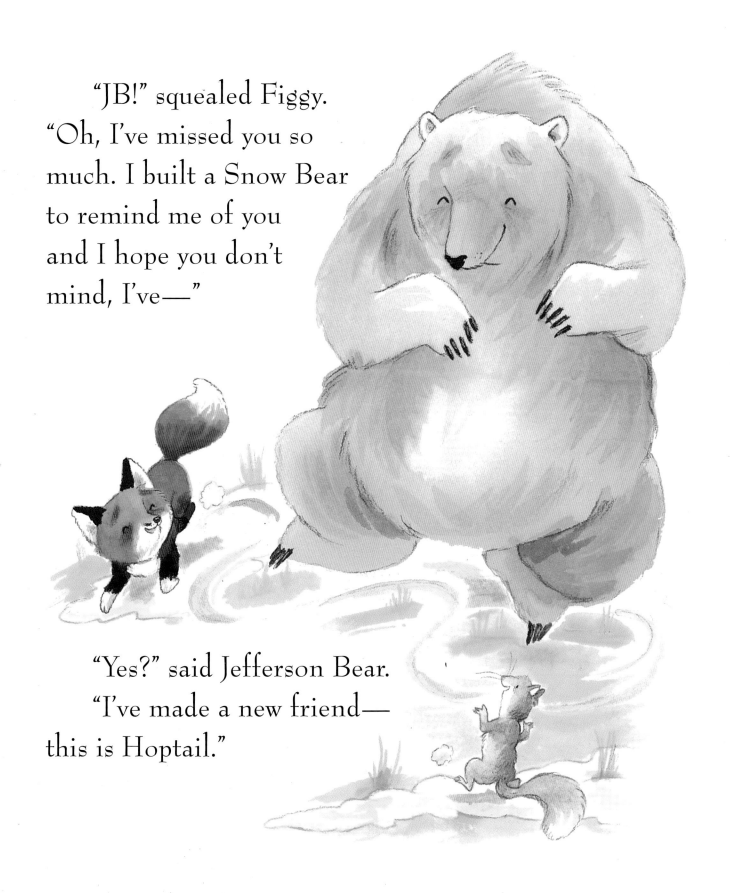

"JB!" squealed Figgy. "Oh, I've missed you so much. I built a Snow Bear to remind me of you and I hope you don't mind, I've—"

"Yes?" said Jefferson Bear. "I've made a new friend— this is Hoptail."

Jefferson Bear laughed. "Slow down, Figgy. Let's all go for a walk and you can tell me just what you did without me."